j817
PH

Phillips, Louis

How do you get a
horse out of the
bathtub?

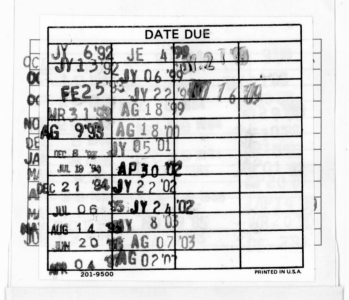

DATE DUE

JY 6'92	JE 4'99	JL 27'99	
JY 13'92	JY 06 '99		
FE 25'93	JY 22 '99	NV 16 '99	
MR 31'93	AG 18 '99		
AG 9'93	AG 18 '00		
DEC 8 '93	JY 05 '01		
JUL 19 '94	AP 30 '02		
DEC 21 '94	JY 22 '02		
JUL 06 '95	JY 24 '02		
AUG 14 '96	MY 8 '03		
JUN 20 '97	AG 07 '03		
APR 04 '98	AG 02 '07		

201-9500

PRINTED IN U.S.A.

© THE BAKER & TAYLOR CO.

How Do You Get a Horse out of the Bathtub?

LOUIS PHILLIPS

How Do You Get a Horse out of the Bathtub?

PROFOUND ANSWERS TO PREPOSTEROUS QUESTIONS

Illustrated by James Stevenson

THE VIKING PRESS, NEW YORK

First Edition
Text Copyright © 1983 by Louis Phillips
Illustrations Copyright © 1983 by James Stevenson
All rights reserved
First published in 1983 in simultaneous hardcover and paperback editions by
The Viking Press and Penguin Books, 40 West 23rd Street, New York, New York 10010
Published simultaneously in Canada by Penguin Books Canada Limited
Printed in U.S.A.
1 2 3 4 5 87 86 85 84 83

Library of Congress Cataloging in Publication Data
Phillips, Louis.   How do you get a horse out of the bathtub?
Summary: Humorous questions and answers in eight categories
parody the suggestions offered by advice columnists.
1. American wit and humor. 2. Wit and humor, Juvenile. 1. Jokes.
2. Questions and answers 1. Stevenson, James, ill. II. Title.
PN6163.P49 1983   818'5402   82-60080   ISBN 0-670-38119-5

This book is dedicated to
Michael Burke
Julie Whittaker
& their daughter Shannon.
I hope it brings some laughs, some smiles.
L. P.

CONTENTS

CHAPTER ONE

...

Questions Concerning Matters Strictly Personal

...

Diet, health, family problems,
financial planning, career advice—
you name it, we tackle it!

My grandparents gave me a dog for my birthday. Unfortunately my dog has no ears. What should I call it?

There's no sense in calling it, since it won't hear you anyway.

I have a very bad cold. My father says that I should drink a large glass of carrot juice after a hot bath. What do you think?

I think that after you drink the hot bath, you will not have any room for carrot juice.

All my friends have electric toothbrushes. I have been using the old-fashioned kind. Do you think I should get an electric toothbrush?

That depends. Do you have electric teeth?

Tomorrow night is our school dance, and I am going on my very first date. Please tell me how long girls should be kissed.

Long girls should be kissed the same way as short ones.

For the past eight months I have been suffering from insomnia. Do you think that my problem is serious?

Well, I wouldn't lose any sleep over it.

Two years ago my parents gave me a camera for Christmas. I have been taking thousands of pictures. If I sent you some of my photos, could you tell me if my pictures are any good or not?

I'm sorry, but I refuse to make snap judgments.

Don't ask me how, but I have a horse stuck in my bathtub. What should I do?

No problem. Just pull the plug out.

My psychiatrist says that I am suffering from klepto-mania. What should I do?

Whatever you do, don't take anything for it.

My neighbor next door is on a very strange diet. He eats nothing but yeast and shoe polish. What do you suppose is going to happen to him?

I presume that each morning he will rise and shine.

April fifteenth is just around the corner, and my father is going crazy trying to deal with the United States Internal Revenue Service. Will you please tell me how he can avoid taxes?

Turn left at New Mexico.

I am losing my memory. What should I do?

Try to forget about the problem.

I am about sixty-three pounds underweight. In short, and in shorts, I am very, very skinny. Please tell me the best way to get fat.

The best way to get fat is to buy it from the butcher.

My mother says I should become a chiropractor. My father thinks I should become a chiropractor. My aunts and uncles want me to become a chiropractor. Tell me, is it difficult work?

> Yes, because chiropractors have to take a lot of back talk.

My little sister watches television sixteen hours a day. Do you think she'll go down in history?

> Not only will your little sister go down in history, I predict that she will go down in arithmetic, English, and geography as well.

I would like to have soft white hands. What must I do?

> Nothing.

I have just inherited twenty tons of peanuts. Should I eat them, or are peanuts fattening?

> Of course peanuts are fattening. Have you ever seen a skinny elephant?

I am compiling a joke book about knitting. Can you give me any suggestions about the kind of material I should include?

> No. I suggest that you write to a nit-wit.

I am thinking about going into the pet-food business. Can you tell me what the main ingredient is in making dog biscuits?

> Collie flour.

Should I buy a cement truck or a garbage truck?

> Buy a garbage truck because it will always be at your disposal.

I am going to have twenty guests for dinner next month. I would like to serve apple turnover for dessert. How can I make an apple turnover?

> Tickle its ribs.

The headwaiter at my favorite restaurant wants to go on a canoe trip with me. Should I take him along?

> No, because if you take him into your canoe, he'll think tipping is allowed.

I am thinking about studying oceanography, but I'm not certain that I have the right kind of personality for it. What kind of person should study oceanography?

A person who likes to explore things in depth.

Three weeks ago my brother joined the navy. Soon he will be shipping out. Please tell me—when sailors are aboard ship, what do they do to get their clothes cleaned?

Sailors simply toss their clothes overboard to be washed ashore.

Lately I have been very tired all the time. What can I do to avoid that run-down feeling?

> To avoid that run-down feeling look both ways before crossing the street.

Do people look good in tight jeans?

> Not the bulk of them.

Do you think I should get a puppy for my sister?

> It sounds like a fair trade to me.

What is the best way to avoid falling hair?

> Jump out of the way.

I keep getting ringing in my ears. What should I do?

> Get an unlisted ear.

CHAPTER TWO

...

Correct English as She Is Spoked and Rotten (and Other Literary Matters!)

I am writing a very long letter to my friend. Can you tell me the longest punctuation mark in the world?

Certainly. The longest punctuation mark in the world must be the hundred-yard dash.

Will you please give me an example of how spacing between words can change the meaning of a sentence?

Gladly. Spacing is very important between words. For example, man's laughter is funny; manslaughter is not.

My grandparents are both librarians. Consequently my parents go around all day with their noses stuck in books. What should I do?

You could buy them some Kleenex.

I don't know much about sports. Can you tell me the exact meaning of tennis?

Two times five? Tennis.

In an old book of proverbs, it is written that "Cleanliness is next to godliness." Do you really believe that is true?

All I know is that grime doesn't pay.

I have recently discovered a literary document written by the Vikings. Can you tell me how I can go about deciphering it?

It is very likely that anything written by Vikings is written in Norse Code.

If you call a group of lions a pride of lions, and if you call a group of cows a herd, what word is used to describe a group of dermatologists, or skin doctors?

A rash of dermatologists will do nicely.

When did people first utter the phrase, "God bless America"?

When America first sneezed.

In an eighteenth-century novel there is a reference to snuff salesmen. Please tell me what a snuff salesman does.

A snuff salesman is a person who goes around putting his business into other people's noses.

Is there another name for income tax?

Some people refer to it as Capital Punishment.

My father is working on a collection of quotations from famous people. We would like to know what Thomas Edison said on the day he invented the light bulb.

Edison didn't say a thing. He was too shocked.

What is the exact difference between a glutton and a hungry man?

A hungry man longs to eat, while a glutton eats too long.

What is the meaning of lumberjack?

Something you use to lift up a flat tree.

I have been studying the Bible for years, but there is one question that I have not been able to get any answer to. Will you please tell me what kind of lights Noah used on his Ark?

He must have used floodlights.

What four-letter word do modern people find most objectionable?

Work.

My mother is a podiatrist. I was thinking of giving her a book for Christmas. What do you suggest?

Whatever book you select, I suggest you pick one that has plenty of footnotes.

Will you please complete the proverb, "If at first you don't succeed . . ."

If at first you don't succeed, you should try playing the outfield.

What do grammarians mean when they say that the word "cold" is both a positive and a negative word?

They mean that sometimes the eyes (ayes) have it, and sometimes the nose.

Can you supply me with the exact meaning of the word "diplomat"?

A diplomat is a person who, when asked what his favorite color is, says, "Plaid."

My art teacher has assigned me an essay about modern art. What do you call people who make sculptures out of Coca Cola bottles?

I'd call them pop artists.

I love the story of Robin Hood, but can you please tell me why he stole from the rich?

> He stole from the rich because the poor didn't have any money.

What is a tongue twister?

> A tongue twister is a saying that tingles your tangue. I mean a saying that tungles your . . . er, it's a twang tungler . . . a tangler that twists your twung . . . Forget it.

I have been told that there is a new book on the market—on the Biblical method of typing. Can you tell me something about it?

> The Biblical method of typing is based on the principle, "Seek and ye shall find."

I know the first half of a famous saying, but for the life of me, I can't remember the rest of it. Can you complete the sentence, "Where there's a will . . ."?

Where there's a will, there is many an anxious relative.

What word is made shorter by adding a syllable to it?

Short.

Is it ever correct to say, "I is"?

Yes, it is. When you say, " 'I' is the ninth letter of the alphabet."

Is there any question that cannot be truthfully answered "yes"?

"Are you asleep?" is one such question. Perhaps our readers can think of others.

What is propaganda?

Propaganda is a socially correct duck.

Is there any two-letter word in the English language beginning with the letter "N"?

No.

I am an English teacher who studies the language of advertising. I have heard my students speak about a product called Beatle soap. What is it?

You put Beatle soap in your bathtub and watch the Ring-O!

What is your opinion of an English teacher who gives all her students "F" on a vocabulary test?

Words fail me.

Is there such a thing as a word in the English language that contains all the vowels?

Unquestionably.

Can you give me some examples of a collective noun?

Three collective nouns come to mind right away—flypaper, wastepaper basket, and vacuum cleaner.

Do you think cook books make good reading?

Some people find such material stirring.

What kind of phrase is "life in prison"?

> To some people that isn't a phrase—it's a sentence.

What is the definition of ignorance?

> I don't know.

CHAPTER THREE

...

Questions
in a Somewhat
Scientific Vein

I am going to the seashore, but I cannot sleep at night there because the sea makes so much noise. Why does the ocean roar?

Because it has crabs in its bed.

Do you know of any invention that allows people to see through walls?

How about windows?

I am a teacher of astronomy, but fewer and fewer students are signing up for my course. Why do you think fewer people than ever before are studying astronomy?

Because the subject is over most people's heads.

*I love summer because the days are so long, but I
don't know why this happens. Can you, in simple
terms for the layperson, explain why days are long in
the summer and short in the winter?*

Days are long in the summer and short in the
winter because heat expands things and cold con-
tracts them.

*I have been fascinated by railroad trains all my life,
but I have been wondering why it is impossible for the
locomotive to sit down. Can you find the answer to
that question?*

The locomotive cannot sit down because it has a
tender behind.

Why is the sky so high?

So the birds won't bump their heads.

*I have been experimenting with different ways of mak-
ing fire. Can you tell me if there is an easy way to
start a fire by using just two pieces of wood?*

It is easy to start a fire with two pieces of wood if
one of those pieces of wood is a match.

*I understand that an inventor has crossed an electric
blanket with an electric toaster. What does his invention accomplish?*

It pops people out of bed in the mornings.

I know that rain falls, but does it ever get up?

In dew time.

Why do ducks go into the water?

For divers reasons, I guess.

Will you please settle a bet? Does lightning ever strike the same place twice?

No. After lightning strikes, the place isn't there any more.

I am a student of biology. My teacher says that cats have nine lives. Does any other animal have more lives than a cat?

A frog has more lives than a cat because a frog croaks every night.

Can you provide me with some inside medical information? What do doctors take to cure the flu?

About thirty to fifty dollars a visit.

*Thank you. That helped a lot. Will you please provide
me with further inside medical information? I mean,
isn't there an answer to the common cold?*

> "Gesundheit" is one such answer.

*In my science class we are studying longevity and the
question of aging. Do you know of any surefire way a
person can live to be one hundred years old?*

> There is only one surefire way. Drink a glass of
> milk every day for 1200 months.

*Can any animal in existence jump as high as the Em-
pire State Building?*

> All animals that can jump can jump higher than
> the Empire State Building, since the Empire
> State Building can't jump at all.

*The other day I found a four-leaf clover, but its leaves
were all wrinkled. Will I harm the clover if I iron the
leaves?*

> Do not iron a four-leaf clover because it is never a
> good idea to press one's luck.

*I have been studying chocolate chip cookies for ten
years, but I cannot understand why cookies crumble.
Do you have any opinion on this important subject?*

> The cookie crumbles because its mother has been
> a wafer so long.

My science fair project requires me to keep high explosives in my home. Do you think it will be all right for me to keep dynamite in my refrigerator?

Not unless you want to blow your cool.

The other day I was walking along the beach and I saw a lot of jelly fish. How does a jelly fish get its jelly?

A jelly fish gets its jelly from the ocean currants.

Which is heavier—a full moon or a half-moon?

A half-moon is heavier because a full moon is lighter.

I am taking my driver's test next week. Will you please tell me what part of an automobile is most likely to cause an accident?

The nut behind the wheel.

Do cows give milk?

    No, you have to take the milk from them.

Please tell me what cowhide is used for.

    To hold the cow together.

Do any animals cry?

    Well, I've seen whale blubber.

How many sheep does it take to make a single wool sweater?

    I didn't know sheep could knit.

What is the major difference between a wild horse and a tame one?

    The only difference between a wild horse and a tame horse is a little bit.

What is quicksilver?

> Those are words used by The Lone Ranger when he is being chased by his enemies.

What time of year do the leaves begin to turn?

> The night before final exams.

What is the best way to prevent infections caused by biting insects?

> Don't go around biting any insects.

Can you explain to me in very simple nonscientific language just what bacteria are?

> I believe that bacteria refers to the rear exit to a cafeteria.

What color is a hiccup?

> Burple.

What is nitrate of sodium?

> Half the day rate.

Please tell me which is more important—the sun or the moon?

> The moon is obviously more important because the moon gives us light at night when we need it, whereas the sun gives us light only during the day when it is already light out.

*I am taking botany, and I am doing extensive re-
search on poison ivy. I plan to cross a poison ivy vine
with a four-leaf clover. What do you think I will get?*

I hope you will get a rash of good luck.

Why does a flamingo stand on only one leg?

If he lifted it, he would fall down.

*I know there are great horned owls, but is there such
a thing as an indifferent owl?*

Yes. An indifferent owl is one that doesn't give a
hoot.

*What happens when a human being is completely im-
mersed in water?*

The telephone rings.

Why do salmon swim upstream to spawn?

> Because walking along the riverbank hurts their tails.

Is a potato the best source of starch?

> No, the best source of starch is probably your local laundry room.

What are the ocean tides called?

> Eb and Flo.

How can I keep a skunk from smelling?

> Hold its nose.

CHAPTER FOUR

...

Around the World
In 80, Dazed

I am a plant collector, and I travel all around the world collecting rare varieties. Where can I go to see man eating plants?

> If you wish to see man eating plants, I suggest that you go to a vegetarian restaurant.

Recently my three cousins and their parents moved to Missouri. Will you please tell me why so many people want to live in Missouri?

> Missouri loves company.

I am going to India for an extended vacation, but I am very afraid of tigers. Is it true that tigers will not hurt you if you are carrying a torch?

> It most likely depends upon how fast you carry it.

*I am going on a trip around the world, and I have
been warned about drinking the water. What kind of
water is healthiest to drink?*

> Well water, obviously. Well water is healthy
> water. At least it's not sick.

Why doesn't Sweden export cattle?

> Because she keeps her Stockholm.

What is the richest country in the world?

> It must be Ireland because her capital has been
> Dublin for hundreds of years.

*I am a band leader, and my band and I have been in-
vited to play in Arabia. Can you tell me something
about dancing in Arabia?*

> The people prefer dancing sheik to sheik.

*I am a very impatient person. Please tell me the best
way to cut my travel time in half.*

> Go half as far.

*Last summer I visited the Petrified Forest in Arizona. I
was wondering if you would tell me (and your millions of readers) just how the Petrified Forest came into
existence.*

> The Petrified Forest came into existence when the
> wind blew so hard that it made all the trees rock.

Where is the Pacific Ocean the deepest?

At the bottom.

When I go to Sweden for the summer, what kind of car do you think I should rent?

Have you considered a Fjord?

I have heard that there is a hotel called The Fiddle. Can you tell me how that hotel received its name?

The Fiddle Hotel received its name because it is a vile inn.

Is it really all right to eat desert sand?

Why eat sand when you can eat dirt cheap?

I am fascinated by the Leaning Tower of Pisa. Can you tell me what makes the tower lean?

> The Tower of Pisa is lean because it doesn't eat very much.

I soon shall be traveling around the world. Will you please tell me three ways to say good-bye to my classmates?

> You can try adieu, adios, and arsenic.

When I travel to Canada, should I go by way of Buffalo?

> You can if you want to, but you might be better off going by way of train or airplane.

I am taking my spring vacation in Mexico this year. What kind of weather can I expect?

> Chili today, hot tamali.

I am going to climb the Rocky Mountains this summer. What should I use to cook my food with?

> If I were you, I would take along a mountain range.

In the Caribbean I have heard of people drinking Bermuda sodas. What are Bermuda sodas?

> You take one sip and your breath comes in short pants.

I want to travel to Europe. Should I take a ship?

> You can take a ship—that is, if you have that much to carry. I feel that you are better off taking a suitcase.

I am going on a picture-taking safari in Africa. Is there any surefire way to prevent a rhinoceros from charging?

> I suggest you take away its credit card.

I will drive through New Orleans next week. What is the proper way to greet the natives?

> How's bayou?

I hate noise and I want to avoid noise at all cost. Will you tell me what is the noisiest country in the world so I can make sure that I don't go there?

> The noisiest country in the world is probably Tibet. Everywhere you go it's yak, yak, yak.

*Will you please tell me your personal opinion of the
Grand Canyon?*

It's just gorges.

*I have lived in the country since I was a baby. I am
now going to New York City for the first time. Please
tell me what kind of time I can expect.*

Eastern Standard.

*I should like to see a real live poet. Is there any spe-
cial place to go to see poets?*

You might try visiting a bard sanctuary.

*I have been asked to spend two weeks on my grand-
father's farm this summer. I will be asked to milk the
cows. Is it easy to milk cows?*

It is very easy. Any jerk can do it.

*Is it a good idea to write ahead to a hotel before trav-
eling to a strange city?*

I have no reservations about that idea.

*I have been bringing back brooms from China. May I
have your personal opinion—which is better: a broom
made in China out of straw, or a broom made in the
United States out of artificial fibers?*

I can't answer that question because I don't like
to make sweeping judgments.

*My sister loves talking on the telephone. Please tell me
in what country it is most expensive to make long-
distance phone calls.*

> Iran, because everyone in Iran calls Persian to
> Persian.

In Africa, what kind of insect is the most annoying?

> I say mosquitoes because they tend to get under
> your skin.

*I was told that while traveling across the Sahara I
should wear a wristwatch at all times. Can you tell me
why?*

> Because every watch has a spring on it.

*For school I am reading John Keats's poem, "Ode to
a Grecian Urn." Please tell me—what's a Grecian
urn?*

> That's a difficult question to answer, but I'd say
> he earns a few hundred drachmas at a bare mini-
> mum.

*I understand that Russia is going to open a new res-
taurant on the moon. Do you recommend that I eat
there?*

> The food may be good, but I know there won't be
> any atmosphere.

CHAPTER FIVE

...

Planning for the Future & Other Things that Nobody Knows Very Much About

I have been invited to become a censor for my local library. Do you think I should take the job?

Not unless you enjoy sticking your "No's" in other people's business.

I have just been elected mayor of a small town in New Mexico, and I need to find out how many thunderstorms our city can expect next year. Whom do you recommend I hire?

I recommend that you hire a lightning calculator.

My dentist is in love with a manicurist. Should they marry?

I don't think it is a good idea that they get married, for it seems obvious that they will be fighting tooth and nail.

Should I give my brother a mule next Christmas?

Why not? He'll get a big kick out of it.

I am decorating my room. What is the most striking object I can purchase in the way of a desk ornament?

A clock . . . or a baseball bat . . . or a match.

I am a young girl, and I am planning to be a dentist when I grow up. Do you think it will be difficult for me to get into dental school?

Getting into dental school always takes some pull.

My brother is going to get married in three months, but he does not have very much money. Please tell me, is it true that two people can live as cheaply as one?

They can live as cheaply as one, but only half as long.

Should I purchase an automobile that has automatic drive?

Of course not. Do you want your friends to think that you are shiftless?

I plan to join the ministry. When I do, will it be important for me to rehearse my sermons?

Yes. It is extremely important for a minister to practice what he preaches.

I have been taking trumpet lessons for the past five years, but now I want to switch to the accordion. What do you recommend?

> No one should play the accordion unless he or she wants to play both ends against the middle.

I have been offered a job in a bowling alley. Do you think I should take it?

> I don't think so. It will pay only pin money.

I have a friend who works as a waiter in a New York City restaurant. He is thinking of running for President of the United States. Do you think waiters make good Presidents?

> It depends on how well they're willing to serve.

My baby sister has a birthday coming up, and she doesn't know how to blow out candles on a cake. I would like to write out instructions for her. How should I begin?

> When it comes to describing how to put out candles, try to give a blow-by-blow description.

My parents are complaining that food prices keep going up—especially the price of steaks and hamburger. Can beef go any higher?

> Certainly. Don't you remember the cow that jumped over the moon?

My mother wants me to work behind a soda fountain this summer. Where should I go to learn the trade?

You might want to attend sundae school.

I am bothered by inflation. Can you tell me why my allowance is not worth as much as it used to be?

I guess dimes have changed.

Since you are good at predicting the future, will you please tell me if the Americans are planning to put some cows into orbit around the earth?

Yes. We want to have the first herd shot around the world.

Should my uncle invest in a store that specializes in skin-diving equipment?

> From what I hear, skin-diving equipment is going under.

Should my optometrist move to Alaska?

> No, because he will only end up as an optical Aleutian.

My brother is joining the army in order to become a paratrooper. I was wondering if you could tell me what will happen if he pulls the cord on his parachute and the parachute doesn't open?

> To answer that question would be jumping to conclusions.

I should like to become a professional flute player.
What should I do?

I think you should find a private tooter.

What happens to football quarterbacks when they get
too old to play the game?

They pass on.

Do you see any change in boys' clothes this season?

I certainly don't see any change in the pockets.

Next year I am going to college, and I am thinking
about studying deserts. What is your opinion?

I think deserts are very dry subjects.

My best friend and I enjoy solving puzzles in newspa-
pers. Do you think we should try to do the puzzles
together?

No. It will only lead to cross words.

Should I become an archaeologist?

No, because your career will soon be in ruins.

I will graduate from high school in two years. Should
I become a professional coffee maker?

Very few people can stand the daily grind.

My eldest son is now a hermit. He lives in a cave. He has, however, written me a letter asking for an automobile. Do you think I should give him an automobile for Christmas?

No. You should not encourage recluse driving.

Lately I've found I cannot keep my mind on my school work. I am thinking about getting a job. I have been asked to go to work for a plant that manufactures frozen orange juice. Do you think that this is a good idea?

There is no sense in going to work for a frozen orange juice plant if you can't concentrate.

CHAPTER SIX
...
Mind over Matter, or the Really Difficult Questions the Experts Dared Us to Answer!

I have a sick pig. Is there anything I can do to help him?

You might try applying some oinkment.

What is mind?

No matter.

What is matter?

Never mind.

Is it true that 3000 unmarried women standing shoulder to shoulder would reach all the way from New York to California?

Yes, it is true because a miss is as good as a mile.

Yesterday my mother and I went to a bowling alley to bowl, and we had to wait four hours. Can you tell me why bowlers play so slowly?

> They play slowly because they have time to spare.

Is trout fishing a disease?

> If it is, it is not necessarily catching.

What makes men mean?

> The letter "A."

Will you please tell me something about the movie The Broken Leg?

> I don't know much about it. All I know is that *The Broken Leg* has a large cast.

How do you make a Maltese cross?

> Kick him in the shins.

I would like to teach my dog a few simple tricks. Is there anything I should know?

> It would probably help if you knew more than your dog.

How can I avoid wrinkles?

> Don't sleep in your clothing.

Please be serious this time. How can I really avoid wrinkles?

> When you see Don Wrinkles coming, walk to the other side of the street.

Why are elephants large, gray, and wrinkled?

> Because if they were small, white, and round, they would be aspirin tablets.

Where can I get dragon milk?

> From a very short-legged cow.

Do you think a six-year-old child should try to climb Mount Everest?

> Of course not. It would be tragic to see a child reach his peak at such an early age.

Will you please explain to your millions and millions of devoted fans the exact difference between Bobby Fischer becoming the United States chess champion at age fifteen and Queen Elizabeth becoming the Queen of England?

> Bobby Fischer was a wonder; Queen Elizabeth is a Tudor.

How do you top a car?

> Tep on the brake, tupid.

Please tell me in what month King Kong was born.

I believe King Kong was born in Ape-ril.

I have a pet elephant, and on a recent sea voyage my elephant became seasick. Is there anything I should give to a seasick elephant?

Plenty of room.

Yesterday I was sitting home all by myself, and I kept hearing the same noise over and over again. Snap, crackle, and pop. Snap, crackle, and pop. What goes snap, crackle, and pop?

A firefly with a short circuit.

Why are so many of the astronauts turned down for regular jobs?

Some of the astronauts are too spaced out.

Will you please tell me what happens to high school principals after they retire.

I think they lose most of their faculties.

Can my parents go insane if they overdraw their checking account?

Well, they will definitely lose their balance.

If I walk on a broken leg, will I suffer a lot of pain?

It depends on whose broken leg you walk on.

Will you please venture a guess as to why Humpty Dumpty had such a great fall?

    I suppose he had a great fall in order to make up for a rotten spring.

On what kind of paper does the United States print its money?

    I think they print it on buckskins.

A few years ago I read a newspaper account about a woman lighthouse keeper marrying a male lighthouse keeper. Have you any information on how their marriage has worked out?

    The last I heard, their marriage was on the rocks.

I have heard that a loaf of bread is a relative of the typewriter. Is that possible?

    Certainly it is. A typewriter is an invention. Bread is a necessity. Necessity is the mother of invention. Therefore, bread is the mother of the typewriter.

How can I make a lemon drop?

    Hold it in your hand and let it go.

Is there any food that is considered "brain food" (I mean food that is good for improving one's brain)?

    Yes, there is. Have you tried noodle soup?

Why is it so difficult for leopards to hide from hunters?

> It is difficult because no matter where a leopard hides, it is spotted.

I would like to study The Lone Ranger's garbage for a paper I am writing. Can you please tell me where The Lone Ranger takes his garbage?

> To the dump, to the dump, to the dump, dump, dump.

Is the man in the moon rich?

> Of course not. He spends all his quarters getting full.

Why do dragons sleep in the daytime?

> I think they sleep in the daytime because they hunt knights.

If George Washington came back from the grave, do you think people would elect him President?

> I don't think he would have a ghost of a chance.

Please supply me with some background information about Mary and Joseph's flight into Egypt.

> I am sorry. I do not know what airline they used.

Will you please explain to me the exact difference between a rhinoceros and a piece of paper?

You can't make spit balls with a rhinoceros.

Is it true that next Christmas Santa Claus's sleigh is going to be pulled by only seven reindeer?

Yes, what you have heard is true. Comet is staying home to clean the sink.

What makes a flying carpet go so fast?

Turban engines.

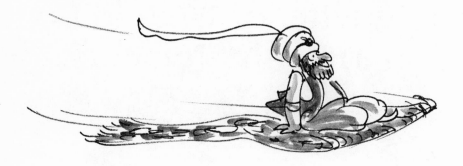

Do you know what is considered to be normal eye-sight for a monster?

20-20-20-20-20-20-20-20.

I am building a pigsty. If I put a lot of holes in the wood, will it make my pigs more intelligent?

Perhaps it will make your pigs litter airy.

What is the major cause of car sickness?

The monthly payments.

CHAPTER SEVEN

...

Etiquette, or What to Do in Ticklish Situations (Even if You Aren't Ticklish)

My life is in danger, and I am looking for a place to hide. What should I do? What should I do? Help!

The best place to hide is inside a mathematics book because there is safety in numbers.

I wish to complain about the high cost of airline tickets. To whom should I write? Perhaps you think it is impolite for me to complain.

You should not complain because it's a fare price that they're quoting.

I have many rich friends and a few poor friends. Can you tell me—is it better to have a rich friend than a poor one?

It is better to have a poor friend, for a friend in need is a friend indeed.

I am throwing a birthday party for some classmates, and I was told to invite several cannibals because cannibals are considered to be the most popular people in the world. Why is that so?

I don't know if cannibals are popular, but I do know they have the most friends for lunch.

Is it correct to mention the number 288 in polite society?

Of course not. It's too (two) gross.

I am planning a birthday party for my father, but I have been told not to invite any workers in the sanitation department because they are very unhappy people. Is that true?

Well, garbage men are down in the dumps a lot.

I own a horse. What is the most gentle spur I can use on it?

Have you tried a whisper?

My aunt is a busybody and is always butting into other people's business. Is there any reason for her to act like that?

Well, your aunt may be suffering from an interferiority complex.

I am giving a graduation breakfast for my sister. Will you please tell me how to make a jelly roll?

Push it downhill.

Do you think it is all right for me to buy a comb from a bald-headed person?

You can certainly try to buy the comb from him, but I doubt that he will ever part with it.

I am giving a formal dinner party for my parents' anniversary. I want to use candles, but I do not know which to use. Which burn longer—round candles or square ones?

As far as I know, all candles burn shorter.

We are doing the play Cinderella. *Can you tell me what kind of gown Cinderella wore to the ball?*

She wore a wish and wear gown.

*If I were running away from the police, where would
be a good place to hide?*

It would be good to hide in a nudist colony because there no one could pin a thing on you.

*There is a mountain that stands between our property
and that of our neighbor. Our neighbor complains
that the mountain gets in the way of his view, and he
threatens to tear the mountain down. What should we
do?*

I think you should call his bluff.

*Every day my eighty-year-old grandmother climbs on
top of her stove and sings cowboy songs. I find this
very embarrassing. Should I make her get off the
stove?*

Of course. Your grandmother is too old to be rid-
ing the range.

I am having guests over to my house for the weekend.
Will it be all right if I cook breakfast in my pajamas?

> It will be fine, but if you are cooking eggs you
> might prefer to use a frying pan.

I have been invited to go ice skating, but I hesitate to
go because every time I go ice skating, I fall down. Do
you think that this will spoil my fun?

> Of course not. Nothing spoils on ice.

I am having dinner at my friend's home next week.
Should I eat fried chicken with my fingers?

> No. You should eat your fingers separately.

Is it good manners to answer questions in a single
word?

> No.

Every time my boyfriend kisses me, he closes his eyes.
Can you please tell me why he does that?

> Send me a photograph, of yourself, and perhaps I
> will be better able to answer that question.

I have been invited to the circus at Madison Square
Garden. On the same day, however, I am also sup-
posed to go to a school dance. What would you do if
you were in my shoes?

> If I were in your shoes, I would polish them.

I would like to give my sister a birthday present worth about $20. What do you suggest?

You could give her a $100 bill.

What should I say to a person who is thinking about stealing an Egyptian mummy?

Tut-Tut.

Do you think it is proper for a young lady to go out with a perfect stranger?

I think it will be very difficult to find a stranger who is perfect.

I have been invited to a formal wedding. What do you think I should wear with my purple and red polka dot stockings?

Hip boots.

After jogging, I am always hot and sweaty. What should I use to clean myself with?

If you are a jogger, you should use running water.

I have a friend who is a basketball player. He is coming to visit me. My problem is this: my friend is seven feet tall, but the bed for him to sleep in is only five feet long. What should I do?

Don't worry, your friend will add two feet to the bed when he gets into it.

*We have moved into a house and have found it to be
filled with cockroaches. What should we do?*

Save them, and if the former owner doesn't re-
turn to claim them in thirty days, you may consider them yours.

*My brother wants to borrow money to buy a ten-speed
bike. Do you have any advice about borrowing
money?*

Tell your brother that if he must borrow money,
he should borrow money from a pessimist. A pessimist doesn't expect that the money will ever be
paid back.

CHAPTER EIGHT

...

A Little Bit of History Goes a Long Way

Where did Napoleon stand when he landed on St. Helena?

He stood on his own two feet.

Someone once told me that the king of Bavaria slept in a bed thirty feet long and twenty feet wide. Is that true?

It sounds like a lot of bunk to me.

According to the Bible, how long did Cain hate his brother?

As long as he was Abel.

What do medical historians consider to be the greatest surgical operation of all time?

Lansing, Michigan.

Where did King Richard III keep his armies?

Up his sleevies.

I am greatly interested in the history of boxing. Please tell me who was the last man to box John L. Sullivan?

The undertaker.

Why did Columbus leave Italy to go to Spain?

I guess Italy was too big to take along with him.

What is the essential difference between George Washington and Abraham Lincoln?

Well, Lincoln lived in Washington, but Washington never lived in Lincoln.

Why was Martin Van Buren born in Kinderhook, New York?

The future eighth President of the United States wanted to be near his mother.

In what way was the sixteenth President of the United States related to Adam and Eve?

Well, the sixteenth President was Abe L.

I am writing the history of gambling. What was the best bet ever made?

I think the best bet ever made was the alphabet.

Who was the first person to make a success in the field of advertising?

> The first great advertiser was Samson of the Old Testament. He took out two columns and brought down the house.

How did Alfred Nobel discover gunpowder?

> The idea came to him in a flash.

In the Bible, why was Goliath so unpopular?

> He was the kind of person who looked down on everybody.

Why is Christopher Columbus considered to be the world's most remarkable salesperson?

> Well, Columbus started out and he didn't know where he would end up. When he got there, he didn't know where he was. When he got back, he didn't know where he had been. Still, he accomplished it all with the help of a sizable cash advance, and he got a repeat order.

Is it true that George Washington tossed a silver dollar across the Potomac River?

> It's true, but you have to remember that a dollar went a lot further in those days.

Why is George Washington buried at Mount Vernon?

> I guess he's buried there because he's dead.

What is the sharpest tool mentioned in the Bible?

> The Acts of the Apostles.

Can you please tell me what ancient mathematicians used instead of paper to write on?

Ancient mathematicians solved their problems on rocks and dirt because they were commanded to multiply on the face of the earth.

I have been studying the Bible, and I was wondering if all the animals that entered the Ark went in pairs.

All except the worms.
The worms went in apples.

I understand that during the Revolutionary War a farmer once trained a chicken to search out British loyalists. I have looked all through my history books and I have read dozens of encyclopedias, but I cannot find the name of that chicken anywhere. Was there ever such a chicken?

Of course there was. You are referring to Chicken Cacciatore. (Chicken Catch a Tory).

In my history book the author claims that the British generals asked to fight the battle of Bunker Hill all over again. What was the reason for the British to make such a request?

> The British felt that the Battle of Bunker Hill wasn't on the level.

Can you settle an argument for me? At what time of day was Adam created?

> Just a little before Eve.

Who was the first person in the history of the world to play tennis?

> Joseph. In the Old Testament, Joseph served in Pharaoh's court.

I have noticed that Moses often wore long robes. Where did Moses get his clothes from?

> Jordan Marsh.

What do I need to be elected President of the United States?

> More votes than your opponents.

What method did Luther Burbank use to grow blackberries?

> Trowel and error.

What do buffalos celebrate every two hundred years?

The Bisontennial.

How did Alfred Nobel feel when he invented dyna-mite?

He got a big bang out of it.

I have been assigned to write a biography of George Washington for my history class. Please tell me for what George Washington is most famous?

His memory. In fact, there is a monument to George Washington's memory right in our nation's capital.

Is it true that Theodore Roosevelt was unfair to horses?

They say he was a rough rider.

When was money invented?

When the dove brought the greenback to Noah.

Captain Cook made three voyages around the world and was killed on one of those voyages. Which one?

Probably the last one.

Louis Phillips, a poet, playwright, and essayist, is the author of more than fifteen riddle and activity books for children. He says that he knew at age seven that he would be a writer, and he has been writing since the second grade. Mr. Phillips received an NEA grant in playwriting. He lives in New York City.

James Stevenson, well-known for his *New Yorker* cartoons, has written and illustrated several award-winning picture books, including *Wilfred the Rat, The Worst Person in the World, The Sea View Hotel* (an ALA Notable Book), and *"Could Be Worse!"* (all published by Puffin Books). Of *"Could Be Worse!"*, a *School Library Journal* "Best of the Best," *The New York Times Book Review* wrote, "After running through one of James Stevenson's easygoing stories you feel he has merely picked up a pen and a box of watercolors and said, 'Hey look—I had the craziest day.'" Mr. Stevenson lives in Connecticut.